Jill,
I miss your
wonderful energy.
winter solstice, 1990.

always, Nora.

Somebody
Should
K I S S
You

BRENDA BROOKS

gynergy books
1990

Cover graphic: Terri Hillstrom
Cover design: Catherine Matthews
Editing & Book design: Lynn Henry
Printing: Les Editions Marquis Ltée

With thanks to the Canada Council for its generous support.

gynergy books
P.O. Box 2023
Charlottetown, Prince Edward Island
Canada, C1A 7N7

Distributed by:
University of Toronto Press
5201 Dufferin Street
Downsview, Ontario
Canada, M3H 5T8

Many thanks to the editors of *Fireweed* and especially *RITES* who previously published some of these poems.

My love to Betty and Cliff for their support of me always. Thank you, Barbie, for taking me on that long drive when I needed it.

My love and thanks also to Barb Richard, Judy Mackay, and Shari Macdonald: Am I half the source of courage and inspiration to you that you are to me?

Thanks to Nancy for every one of our important talks about "working."

Much warmth and affection to Lee Fleming for her open and spontaneous encouragement of this book, and for showing me the ocean.

My appreciation to Lynn Henry for being so nice to a novice and for her thoughtful editing of this book.

Canadian Cataloguing in Publication Data

Brooks, Brenda, 1952-
Somebody should kiss you

Poems.
ISBN 0-921881-12-6

I. Title.

PS8553.R66S65 1990   C811'.54   C90-097648-9
PR9199.3.B76S65 1990

Contents

] you, I am willing [
] suffering [
] and I, for myself [
This I knew something about [
[   ] for them [

SAPPHO

Anything

I can be
your man, I can
be your mother,
I can be

your reluctant nun,

or your favourite
amphibian, fluent
on land or water.

I can be
the girl with
couldn't-care-less-hair
who galloped her
best horse into
the schoolyard &
won your marbles
fair and square.

We could be
dirty & twelve
again, find some
trouble to be up to,
invent our own
words for things —
we could tell
them to each other
in the pungent,
private places
girls like us

(tree girls,
river girls,
girls with pine-cones
on their minds,
who tell time
by the sun, who
find their bearings
by the stars,

restless girls
whose bikes have hooves,
girls with bows
& arrows they made
themselves,
girls with
the sounds of horses
in their throats)

always find.

Fluent on land
or water,
we could be
man, or
mother.

Rumours

It's no secret
everywhere we go
everybody knows

in the city
where the sun
goes down on the
broken flower pots
cluttering the balcony

and on the
lonesome fig tree
leaning toward the window

In the country
where the moon pours
herself through deep
cedar woods

and floats
in the forgotten
rain barrel,
soft green insides
steeping by the door

everyone knows

how filled I am
with wanting her
how it flows down
the sides of things

the moon sinking
slowly into me

MOTEL

You make me think of
long days and nights driving
through a hot, lush state

the watermelons voluptuous
bursting to split
offering their engorged pink
their sweet water
from the roadside.

You make me remember
the way moss clings so tight
to certain stones,
the lobes and blossoms and
purple hues of things,
the throb and syncopation
of the tropical insect chant.

You take me back
to apples at night
ripening in their bowls
beside a southern window,
the red-rimmed, rainy moon
and the drenched whisper
of your rude secrets.

The way your fingers
broke into me
like a ripe peach.
The way you spread your-
self and staggered small,
moist kisses over my thighs,
my stomach, my breasts,
the sliding flutter of you
on my tongue,
the taste of your spices
on my lips.

If I buried this
desire for you deep
in the ground beside a
dried up motel in a dusty
tumbleweed place,
suddenly it would rain
and stay wet
all the purple night.

I Don't Want You

to love me
to uneasy
depths,
(echo of
stone tumbling
down a dry
well)

just come
to me as you
would come to a place
you think you might
like to return
to — maybe
in the fall or
late July or
when the cinnamon ferns
are at their
best.

Come to me
as you come
to a place that whispers
removal of clothing,
that licks the hair wet
on your neck,
place of hard &
soft, of cool
leaves and soft
rushes,
of small sips
from cupped
hands,
of plunging
drinks for the
whole body's
thirst,

slow,
waiting, mid-
summer place of
fully-opened things,
& smooth crevices
gradually, gradually
widening.

If Only

Come to me
soon because I
feel the greedy
nudge deep
between my legs —
take me
between your
fingers,
hurry this
hungry cunt snail
doing its slow
mean thing
there.

Come to me
& bring the
soft chant your hips
sang against my
thigh

quick
breath intake
& sticky glide
& tug of tongue
deep resounding
fuck of your
mouth by
mine.

Come to me
with the kiss
re-defined, the
moment long
awaited, sweet
sear of your
fingers, incurable
pyromania of your
hands

or,

bring me a
sliver for my
heel, a
wasp for the
bedroom,
ice for next
year —

turn this
place on its
end & watch
everything I'm
sure of slide out
the front door

or

(if only
you would)

bring me
the solace of
your
body.

Where Will all Your Good Intentions Be Then?

What if
one evening she
walks into your
favourite café
just when you're getting
serious with Jane Bowles
in a badly lit corner,
and what if
she's wearing
a sensual earring
and two hot colours
and (on top of that)
a scarf filled with connotations
the likes of which
a scarf never had before,
and suppose
your wrists begin to itch
and you hear yourself
gladly having the waiter clear
away the remains of your
dignity and purpose to
make room for her,
and then you sit there
not listening to a thing
she says because the vital thing
is to watch her mouth move,
and also her hands
when they borrow your fork
so she can taste some of
what you're eating —
and then it's back
to her mouth again,
her lips closing softly
on this cool metal
for which your own lips
have new respect —

and what if
she suggests you both
rise to leave
and in doing so takes
your arm into hers
(the way someone takes
something to themselves which
belongs to them unquestionably)
saying something (some
small thing perhaps)
that makes you understand
for the first time
the very fine distinction
between the profane
and sacred — where will

all your frugal purchases,
your neatly-tied packages,
and all your good intentions
be then?

Mess

for Lee

since
she came

everything
drips a churning
rhythm

low
repeat of
percussion i
can barely
stand

saxophones
in the trees
and i

no
longer
understand
cutlery or
buttons

the small
efficient items
of civilization
that keep us
from coming
apart

that keep us
from the messy
wetness of
ourselves

since
she left

i feel
the need
to gulp from
a thick jug
the colour of
earth

the need
for overflow
for wet chin
& damp open
shirt

for hands
persuasive &
primeval

i feel
the need
to crouch &
dig for
something secret &
precious
in the deep muck
under a crazy tree
on a frantic
night

I Want You

to want me
to miserable
excess

obvious

(to
even
the most
distracted
passerby)

your bed
chaotic
nightly

your tongue
tied up

your shocked
friends

this wall
harder
than your
back has
known

don't
love me
sweetly
or get warm
& reassured
when you
see me

instead
wake up
alone
dreaming
lava

I want you
to know
how that
feels

Help me

My mind's a slum
about you honey

all my wants
every one of my dirty,
hungry Wants sit half-naked
around the kitchen table
moaning, never
satisfied.

Tell me
what to do
because i feel
so underprivileged
around you baby
my bedroom's regional
disparity my back yard's
a mess.

If only you'd
motor by sometime
have a look at my
standard of living,
how filthy i am with
conspicuous desire,
(how deprived of ego)
how sticky with sexual id.

What wouldn't i do
to move in close
to get some
intimate grime
on you.

What wouldn't i do
to smear that skillful
lipstick with my
teeth.

So tell me
what to do because
it's nearly December
and i'm still too hot
to hold a job,

give me counsel
show me your reason/
triumph over my passion

do some work
of a social nature
with me
soon,

help me.

Reckless Pennies

Just tell me when I've
said too much — I'll write
you a thin poem re: too little,
using the word Wraith. Just give
me a hint, look away, close the
window, signal the dog. Say no more.
I'll show you Furtive. Practice
the art of concealment every night
till my fingers hurt. Be the guy
with no ticket hiding
in the toilet. Be the quiet vagrant
I know I can be. Or a
better politician. Even though
I know I'm a wide-out verbal slut
who just can't keep her lips together.
But say the one word and I'll fade
to grey, get respectable, try for that
job at the bank, swear to secrecy of
all combinations. Hoard these words,
my reckless pennies, learn to say everything
in the space of a dirty postcard. Sign my
name with one letter. B.

Oh

this thing i have for her mixes me up and makes me
so nervous i want to stop aching like this and for
her to go away i want to ache this way always and
never be left in peace i want to find a short
strand of her hair on my white sweater i want to
watch her eat the froth from the top of her café
au lait let me feel my nipples harden against hers
and tease her and give in please let the insides
of my lips be worn from her kiss i want to pull her
to me and drink until i gasp i want to see her
eyes darken with desire and her anger turn to passion
i want to get it easy i want to take it hard i
want to be kind i want to be bad i want my bathrobe
to slip from her shoulders in the morning i will
make love to her taste every part of her i will
take her taste and texture her most intimate scent-
into-me Oh
        this thing i have

I Wish She

She's so busy
lifting things fixing
things dropping things
off   busy making sure
things not to be
cared about are ready
on time   so concerned that
            there
this is one thing will
never leak again   yes
it's watertight for sure now
even though all I want
is wet   is hotsprings and
slide my hand into
her pocket
maybe find something blue
there saying
water water water   yes but
she's so busy rushing to put
things right   I wish she
            would rush into me
put me right

Stay in touch

Write me a letter
saying you want
to show me
the ocean,
saying my hands
were made for
anemone and pink starfish,
the insides of
intricate shells
which can be made
to moan when you
hold them to
your lips, or
heavy sponges
their deep amber chambers
so seductive to
the fingers

saying my hands
were made for things
softer to the touch
than what even
the greatest lakes
have to offer —
when I arrive
(soon after)
kiss me in an
overly familiar manner,

the next evening
let your body move
over & over
mine like
the tide.

terminus

she says she's good
at goodbyes &
i believe her,
not knowing exactly
what she means but
knowing for sure
she's good at other
things she puts her mind
or lends her hands to —

so i drop her
off for the 5:25
& start back right away
knowing the last thing
she needs is me
to wave her goodbye
or watch the punctual bus
disappear into the
rain —

half-way back down
65 i refuse to let that soulful
song the wipers sing
get to me — i think
about the things she put
her mind to, her head
and how she's kept it,
the lending of her hands —

& i can't think
of a single reason why
this goodbye shouldn't be
as good as any of her others

About emptiness

Night comes back
and the snow
begins carefully,
each quiet flake
placed as if
it knew, as if
there really was
such a thing as
True, such a thing
as Careful

& the trees begin
to cry in mournful
tangled voices, in
their brittle expertise

about emptiness

the return of the
wide white places
that drift

not the way
your hand drifted over
my hip in the dark
but the way

we are now
your back to me
we listen to the lake
exhale and begin
to freeze
under the stars

the cold sigh
of ice on ice,
the singular sound
of a thin, tense crack
shooting through the
surface

now
all I want
to know is if
you heard it too.

She Did

I asked her
to open herself
for me
and I made
my mouth
wait

a mouth
waiting, faltering

softly watering

(poor enamel
cup left in
the rain)

a mouth
waiting,

while someone
you want (slow
hands, silver ring)
peels something sweet
until you have to
swallow

I asked her
hands to do
the soft unfolding
and I made
my mouth
wait

and I touched
my lips to her ring
only   her deep
pink against my
cheek

and I asked her
to lift herself
to me

(full purple cup
offering its fine
eager rim to
drink from)

and I asked her
to ask   and I
made my mouth
wait

and I asked
her to invite me
(precisely)
to drink

& she did

If You Say So, Never

You should have
told me this
was the sort
of dinner where
one pushes
the other away
like an empty
plate, the
sort of dinner
where nothing
is taken in
or savoured,
only got
rid of, made
to disappear

you should have
warned me
about your
illusive eyes,
your careful
married hands,
the hacked-up
memories &
official version
of events
concocted to
explain why
you once
wanted

my kiss.

If I read
you right,
then maybe
my hands never
eased into
your steeping
sex,

never sank
into that
deep eager
loam of
you, I

never knew
the long
line of
your arched
neck reaching
for that
lonely
ecstatic
moment,
your lost
eyes trying
for something
irrevocable &
far, if

I'm getting
the gist
of a
mouth I
thought I'd
know
anywhere,

never
did you
whisper a
fine rain, a
blue forest
into
me.

Unsay.

So then
the jolt
of sudden repossession.
The coming back
to self again.
Re-entering the
room.
This time without
the need. With
rain in your
eyes.

This chair is
a well-known place.
This table. Blank
oblong of bed.
Memory of desire
leans in the shadow.
A red kite
you could have
sworn on.

Everything is less
magic. More
resistable than
you imagined

each thing being
reversible.
Soft reversal of
a whisper her lips own
again from your
ear.

The joyful
skipping stone.
Untouches. Untouches. Untouches.
The fragile skin
of pond.

Please. Please. Please.

I return these
words to you.
Three clear pebbles
dropped without click
or tiny kiss
into an open
hand.

PLEASE

Some things I've
begged you for
don't embarrass me
at all
and never will
like please
don't stop yet don't
get up and stand
so deadly quiet
at the window
your eyes
far away
watching the last
wild apples fall
into the tall grass.

Say something
to stop this procession
of long dark
realizations
one behind the next
ominous limousines
taking me somewhere
I'm not ready
to go.

Please
let on this
isn't happening
something I only
thought I saw
from the corner
of my eye
just one of
those things
that happens
sometimes and
is gone.

You (me)

You
forgetful you
of our happiness
its fat melon
its juicy conspiracy
its long eyes between us
and lure of blissful tongue —
you of the sensual politic
you of the singular interest
you of the midnight candle
by the bed and tips of fingers
deepening, you
forgetful you

& me
now me of the list
of hollow things —
the room after
the thief, the wall
i want to beat on
my heart
me of the dark
planet whose storms
could last
a hundred years
me of the poor
brown coat
a question in
every pocket —

what
what have i done
& what have i
done

HORROR STORIES

That the sun will soon go out,
that you are getting smaller every day,
that your closet hides a pair of yellow eyes,
that the neighbours have sharp teeth and pale children,
that half your friends are the walking dead.

That long ago you foresaw the terrible deaths
of several girls you could have sworn you knew
and you can't stop seeing where the bodies lie,
legs still spread, torn among the early summer daisies.

That you will not be permitted love
without the court's approval, that you will be
arrested by men with yellow rubber hands,
that your scent is latex and your sex synthetic.

That help is always just a bit too late,
that your throat cracks and they
throw you a few dry stones,
that their eyes move over you like
quick, tiny claws. And

your mouth aches
for a kiss,

and the sun is certainly going out,
and you are getting smaller,
and half your friends

Forgive

Forgive me, Mother
for wanting you always,
for wanting to play
quietly at your feet
with my flannel giraffe,
my plastic hammer, my little
gun. Forgive my first small
obscenity. My tiny pink
flower in front of the guests.
Forgive my greed. My wanting
everyone to go home and leave us
together. Forgive
my awkward, skinny jealousy,
my bony thievery. Forgive me
for looting your sewing box.
For stealing the
red button. For slipping it deep
into my cheek like a bit of sweet
candy from you. Like a tiny inflamed
pearl of love and holes.
Forgive me for being lost.
For making you come find me.
For wanting to be the only one
on your knee in the picture. For being
so bad you had to touch me. For
being so wild you couldn't touch me.
Forgive my dirty hands, how they
came back soiled from marbles
or twigs or the arc of powerfully
imagined arrows.
The skinned hands of my ten years
dipping into your dresser drawer
to cup the seductive essence of you;
the nutmeg, the teak, the lavender.
My secret hands on your
intimate silk, your vials of amber,

your Shalimar, your pastel wands,
the delicate chiming of your
music box.
                    Mother, forgive
my lies; the denied and missing things
I held close to myself at night,
the charmed artifacts of you I
pressed to my child's body hoping
for good magic and simple love.
The red button, the stolen earring,
the necessary amulet caressed inside
the pocket, against evil and despair,
against the long disorientation of the first sudden day without
you.

Accepting What is Offered

Wanting you
always

having you
never —

I'm kind to myself
late into the
night

& afterwards:
the same dream
of wild strawberries —

whole fields offering
their fullest tongues,
their reddest kisses

(their heaviest
hearts)

to me.

Home

(for Laura, whatever her name)

I saw you on the bus
the day I bought the book
on Patagonia, because
of its beech forests
& black-necked swans,
its sea lions perfectly
at home on the Valdez Peninsula,
because of its austral
parakeets & mention of
a south wind.
         I saw you
and it all came back:
the jittery circumstances
under which we met, the sudden
accumulation of friends who
couldn't cope, who played
euchre until bedtime, smoking
too much, waiting for
the medication trolley and
its compulsory dessert,
(something delicate & sweet
especially for you.)

         Who could blame us if
there were times we longed
to overdo it &
did?

It all came back: the way
you sat, your chin turned in
toward the heel of your hand,
your perpetual left knee,
the desire in your eyes
for a deep & lasting
faint.
         This was the season we lost
possession of ourselves,

the season of un-infatuation, of
spiders & anxiety. The
time of distracted hands
& shadows of dry, lifeless
things blowing by the
window.

         At night
a thousand town criers
filled my head & the news
wasn't good.

         In the morning
you & I grimly acquiesced
to our occupational hour:
another coloured tile,
another shade added to our
aching to be
gone.

Laura —
         Now I've put your
name, my ache, in the same
place — away from me.
         To find the place
where I could be at home
again. Not the place we knew,
where a woman could slip away
in her nightgown and blue slippers
and not be seen again;
where small amounts
were offered, measured
from the tips of
fingers.
         To remember
the place where the deer come
down in their grey grace
to drink again; where fish
throw themselves from the river,
heavy with silver need, and

the river opens its long, clear
arms to take them back
again.

Your face
turned in toward the
heel of your hand when
I saw you on the bus and
it all came back —
the day I bought the book
on Patagonia, because
of its beech forests
& black-necked swans,
its sea lions perfectly
at home, because of
its austral parakeets
& mention of a south
wind.

Magicicada Singing

Deep July
hot night

the last
ice in the
glass.

Out there
clinging to a
twig, a brick
wall —

I know
life is lonely
for the cicada

only something
perishable & lonely
would wail
so

the longest please,
a deafening
prayer to
the stars
I have also
prayed to:

Let me
fulfill the
brief occasion

please

after so much
time preparing

give to me
each one
of my few
magic weeks.

Wish

for Judy

I.

If I had known
you at thirteen
would you have shared
with me all the secrets
you knew (and I did not)
about loss,
about cruelty,
about being shoved around,
about being made to do?
Would you have shown
me the special tricks
you learned: how to
disappear quickly,
how to avoid being alone with
certain people,
how not to cry
so easily?

In return
would I have
given you a
broken watch, a
pocket knife, two grey
feathers from someone
who floated high over
everything,
a wish buried
under a secret tree?

II.

I wish for you
a warm rock
like the one we
swam from at Stoney Lake:
cedar for shade,
careful entrance into
deep green,
you naked
except for your flippers;
so strange and lovely a sight,
even the fish came out,
their mouths amazed,
to watch you fly
over their
houses.

History

We shall have a house in the woods
with a roof so blue it can be seen
from the road. And not only a house —
a dark shed filled with dust and
creaking angles of light when entered.
And things hanging up — a sled, a saw.
Pieces of leather and warm brass.
Lamps that swing from our fingers
when we cross the yard under the new
moon. A box filled with petrified
wood and fossils. A box we are filling
with murmurs and whispers and clues —
the fragmented story of your defiant
hands, the deep impression of your kiss.
Be assured of this — though they insist
later that we never lived here — be assured
that all about will be the stubborn clutter,
the undeniable record, the burning, wilful
evidence speaking you and me into eternity.

Don't Touch Her

for Shari

It would be
a mistake to assume,
because you see her
there (alone) where
the burrs cluster to her
with their fine hooked
fingers and she
doesn't notice,

because you see
her there (alone)
where she makes
her careful pictures
of rock & lichen as
they've never been seen
before, where
her eyes are so
obviously distracted by
such matters as
shadow & light,

it would be
a mistake to assume,
because you see her
there (alone),
that you
should touch
her —

Because, listen:

I have a
rough shirt & strong
shoulders, nothing
stops my feet gliding
through this forest
(with her); my
skin the scent
of mushroom, my hair

the dark undersides
of moss lifted from
a tree, my voice
the replacing of this
moss quietly —

It would be
a mistake to assume —

because I belong here
(with her) my
hands are understood
by wood & water,
my sex is cypress and wind;
and the soft pouch I've
fastened around her neck,
warm against her breast,
is the exact size
of my heart.

Somebody Should Kiss You

for Barb

Somebody should kiss you
when you do that

when you play so rough
with your eyes

when your voice is too low
to be fair

every word a heat-
crazed bee
working a hot field

every one of your laughs loaded
with honey and dust.

Everything you do
turns my stomach high voltage.

You make me so sick baby
when you turn and sweep that
excruciating chemistry from your hair;

somebody should kiss you
when you do that.

Attending the Ceremony

First of all I was
going to wear a skirt because
she thinks my legs are something
else and likes to help me un-
cross them slowly after we get home
but then we didn't want to seem
to be playing roles even though we
do sometimes so we both wore pants
and I picked that shirt I bought
for the last dance and she dragged
out that bra brooding in her
bottom drawer for oh
a long time now and I laughed
until she made me stop.

Later in the church
she sat so unpiously close
a broken commandment couldn't
come between us and each time
she moved was the dizziness of
slightly warm perfume
the distraction of her fingers
slipping beneath the blue
water's edge of her blouse
the distraction of her lips
moistening that small pink stone
at her throat the distraction
of a small pink stone moistening
the ceremony of her lips moving
over it like a prayer slowly
after we got home.

Hide your Hands

I wonder

how long can
your hands go
on this way
before being seized
& held at the
border.

Whose eyes
will be first
to guess
your hands are
witches,
wizards to light
the night
horizon,
conjurors
conspiring by fires
beyond the limits
of town where long
trains make their
lonely run
for it.

I worry

how long can
this go on,
knowing your hands
are two ideas
most obscene,
more dangerous
than nipples.

Even now

quietly spreading
the lips of
your book —

your fingers
are something
to be reckoned with,
cause for
consternation,
reason for
concern.

So I wonder

will they come
for you soon
with wrought-
iron eyes,
their cool, barbed
fingers & keen
interrogative
manner.

Hurry

before the dark
van in the
street,
before the
boor on the
stair —
hide your hands
on me.

Under these Circumstances

When they dig deep for what is considered
the most horrifying adjective,
when they come onto you in the street

when they tell you
(and they will tell you)
that you are a sick cunt
and perverted bitch whose dyke face
they would like to (in so many words)
smash

when they invite you
to suck them off —

it will be important to remember

the night the rain came through the window
and you licked the drops from her shoulder
and they were sweeter than the ripe,
wet pears glowing in the grass

how you woke up longing,
wanting this woman too much;
how she could make you suffer in the dark
whether or not she was there.

Try to recall the way her voice broke
when you touched her just the right way,
how learning to touch her the right way
was all that ever mattered.

Bring back your own nakedness
against her rowdy jeans, her torn
sweatshirt stained red & green,
the way she held your wrists
as you strained to come.

Under these circumstances
it will be an inspiration to recall
her Fuck Off walk, perfected
in cruel streets
and other corridors of ridicule,
all meaningless to you now that you
no longer fear the rain coming through the window:

lick the drops from her shoulder.

Save me a Place

Honey you
are so.

The Event of the
Year, a festival of
lights,

seventeen days
of merriment & abandon,
Queen of Hearts &
Laughter.

How will I
find a spot
high enough to
view you?

You deserve
your own drum
& majorette —

I'm telling
the Mayor
on you —

the keys
to the City,
the day re-named,
the night &
the trumpets lengthened.

Yes you are
the most
outrageous float
in the Parade
(you told me so)

for sure someone
was up all night
working on you.